W9-ARZ-827

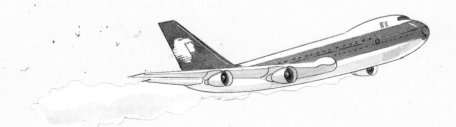

A LANGUAGE LEARNING ADVENTURE

GOODBYE USA
¡Hola México!

Anne Elizabeth Bovaird
Spanish version by Harriet Barnett
Illustrated by Pierre Ballouhey

BARRON'S

"Scat cat, I'm trying to read!" said Tom looking at a picture book of Mexico City.

"Listen to this, Mom, the book says that Mexico City is very old and there are lots of interesting things to see. For instance, there is a big park called Chapultepec Park with lakes to row on and a museum in it, and a big square called a plaza with buildings around it and even a palace! It's called the Zócalo."

Next week Tom is going to Mexico City to visit his cousin Pablo, Aunt Margarita, and Uncle Juan for the first time. Tom's dad is taking the plane with him as far as Mexico City. Then he is leaving Tom to go to an important business meeting.

"Does cousin Pablo speak English like me?" Tom asked, looking at a picture of Pablo and his family. He wondered what they would be like.

"Why no, Tom. Pablo's Mexican and he speaks Spanish."

"You mean he doesn't know any words in English! How can we be friends if I don't understand what he says!" Tom hadn't thought of this before now, and he was nervous about meeting someone he couldn't talk to.

"Not everyone in the world speaks English," Tom's mom continued.

Tom of course knew that. He knew kids at school who spoke Spanish. But he wasn't sure about making friends with someone from another country.

"Tell you what—I'll teach you some words in Spanish. After all, Pablo's the same age as you. You have lots of things in common. I'll write down some expressions in English and what they mean in Spanish next to them," she said taking a sheet of paper and a pen.

Tom sat down with his mom at the desk.

"First of all, what do you notice about the English words and the Spanish words?"

Tom looked at the list long and hard. A lot of words looked different, but some looked familiar. "Well, the word 'no' is the same in Spanish and *avión*, the Spanish word for 'plane', looks like 'aviation'."

"That's right," Tom's mother agreed. "Some words do look the same but they're pronounced differently. Let's draw a third column. When I say the word in Spanish, you tell me what it sounds like in English."

"The first word is *Hola*. It means 'Hi.'

"O-lah," repeated Tom. "Well, the first part sounds like the letter O and the second part like the musical note 'lah.' But you said the O a little louder." "Very good! So let's write 'O-lah.' We'll use a capital to remind you to pronounce it just like the letter O, and we'll make it a little darker to remind you to say it a little louder than the lah.

"I get it! And I'll just pretend the H doesn't exist!"

English	Spanish	Sounds like
Hi	Hola	**O**- lah
How's it going?	¿Qué tal?	Keh - tal
Fine	¡Bien!	B- N
Good bye	Adiós	ah - D - **os**
Good day	Buenos Días	Boo - EH - nos **D**- ahs
Thank you	Gracias	**grah** - C - ahs
Please	Por Favor	**pore** - fah - vore
Yes	Sí	see
No	No	no
Plane	Avión	ah - V - on
Aunt	Tía	T - ah
Uncle	Tío	T - O
Cousin	Primo	**pree** - mo

"That's right. Now the second expression is *¿Qué tal?* It means 'How's it going?' You answer it with *Bien*, 'fine.' It's a kind of greeting used between two friends. What does it sound like in English?"

"The first part sounds like keh and the second like tahl. Say them together fast— **keh**-tahl and they mean 'How's it going?' in Spanish! And I answer back *B-N*. Things are great!'"

Tom was quite happy with himself. Spanish isn't half as complicated as he had feared—And if you practice along with him, you can learn some Spanish too!

"Okay. So now I know a few expressions in Spanish," explained Tom. But what about all the other words I don't know? What do I say when I want to know what something is in Spanish? Pablo's going to think I'm stupid!"

"No he won't," laughed his mother. "When you want to know what a word is in Spanish, just ask him. 'What is it?' in Spanish is *¿Qué es?* "

"**K** S," repeated Tom. "That's really easy! Okay, now it's my turn. Let me try to speak Spanish," said Tom excitedly. "*¿Qué es*, Mom? See this model airplane Dad gave me? It's a big 747 jet, like the one I'm going to take tomorrow."

Tom's mother laughed. His enthusiasm pleased her.

"The word plane is *avión* in Spanish. *Es un avión* means, it's a plane."

"S oon ah-V-**on**. Hey, I'm speaking Spanish!"

"And this is a present for your *Tía Margarita*. In Spanish, a present is *regalo*," said Tom's mom.

"Reh-**gah**-lo. *Es un regalo*," sang Tom. "It's a present!"

The night before his trip, Tom went to bed dreaming about Mexico. He wondered what Mexican kids do for fun. Do they have toy trains and racing cars? Do they ride bikes and roller skates? Do they play baseball?

The new Spanish words he had learned ran round and round in his head. See if you can match the Spanish words with the English.

The next day Tom woke up and went down for breakfast.

"*Buenos días*, Mom," he shouted. "*¿Qué tal?*"

"*Buenos días*, Tom. *Bien, gracias,*" answered his mom. She was fixing a special meal before his trip. "After breakfast we'll finish packing, and I'm going to take an *avión*, and give *Tía Margarita un regalo*, and say *Qué tal* to Pablo, and . . ."

"Not so fast! Finish your breakfast first," said Tom's dad.

At the airport, Tom had to show his passport at the ticket counter. His passport says that he is American and was born in Chicago.

The woman who took his ticket explained that the plane ride was about four hours long and that Mexico City was 1,686 miles (or about 2,700 kilometers) away. The plane had to fly over Missouri, Arkansas, Louisiana, and the Gulf of Mexico before arriving at Benito Juarez Airport in Mexico City.

When it was time to get on the plane, Tom suddenly felt sad. He put his arms around his mother and gave her a big hug.

"Be good, Tom," said his mom. "And remember, Pablo is just like your friends back here in Chicago. Call me tomorrow night when you arrive."

"*Sí*, Mom. I will. *¡Adiós!*"

"*¡Adiós Tom!*"

Tom and his dad placed their bags on a conveyor belt to be X-rayed.

"Security checks are very important," Tom's dad explained.

On the plane, the flight attendant gave Tom a landing card to fill out. The attendant said he would have to give this to the immigration officer in Mexico City. All foreigners traveling to Mexico are required to do this. Tom had never thought of himself as a foreigner before.

The card was written in both Spanish and English and some of the Spanish words looked familiar. For instance, "name" and *nombre*, "nationality" and *nacionalidad*, "occupation" and *ocupación*.

Tom remembered what his mom said about some Spanish words looking like English words. "Boy, she sure knows a lot!" he thought.

At the Benito Juarez Airport, Tom said good-bye to his dad. He was so excited to be in Mexico that he forgot to feel sad!

Tom followed the other passengers to the immigration counter and waited his turn. "*Buenos días*," said Tom to the officer behind the counter.

"*Buenos días*," answered the man without looking up. He took Tom's landing card and stamped his passport.

"*Adíos*," said Tom.

"*Adíos,*" said the man.

"I did it," thought Tom. "I spoke Spanish and he understood me!"

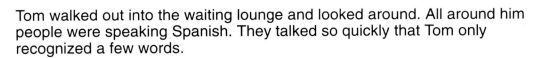

Tom walked out into the waiting lounge and looked around. All around him people were speaking Spanish. They talked so quickly that Tom only recognized a few words.

"I'm not afraid of all these people," thought Tom. But he was, just a little.

"Hey wait a minute! There's someone holding up a sign with my name on it!"

"¡*Bienvenido Tom!* I'm your *Tía Margarita.*"

"B-N-veh-**nee**-doe?" repeated Tom.

"That means, Welcome. We're so glad you could come to Mexico City!" *Tía Margarita* speaks English. What a relief!

"*Tía Margarita, es un regalo,*" said Tom, holding out the present his mom gave him.

"*Ay Tom, gracias.*"

"This is your cousin, *Pablo*, Tom."

Tom looked at Pablo.
Pablo looked at Tom.

He looks like an ordinary kid, Tom thought. He's even the same size as me. Only difference is he's got dark hair. Also, he's wearing glasses and is all dressed up.

"*Hola, Tom. ¿Qué tal?* " asked Pablo politely.

"*Hola, Pablo, bien gracias*!" answered Tom.

Tom held out his hand to Pablo . . .

All of a sudden, Pablo reached over and hugged Tom.

"Hey, cut that out!" said Tom. "I'm not a girl!"

Pablo looked hurt. "*Lo siento, Tom*," he said.

"Lo **C**-N-toe?" repeated Tom.

"*Lo siento* means I'm sorry, Tom. We often hug members of the family when we meet," explained *Tía Margarita*. "Pablo just wanted you to feel welcome."

"I . . . I'm sorry," Tom said. "You see, we don't do that in Chicago. We usually just shake hands."

Tom held his hand out again to Pablo. He felt terrible. He hoped Pablo didn't think he was mean or unfriendly.

But Pablo didn't seem to mind. He took Tom's hand and smiled.

On the way from the airport they drove on a beautiful avenue with flowers and modern-looking buildings as well as impressive old buildings. Tom thought he recognized it from somewhere. Well, the only way he was going to find out was by asking.

"*¿Qué es, Pablo?*" said Tom, hoping Pablo understood him.

"*Ah Tom, es el Paseo de la Reforma*," answered Pablo.

"S L pah-**seh**-O deh lah reh-**for**-mah. I get it! Now I remember. It's *el Paseo de la Reforma*. I saw it in the picture book I have about Mexico City."

Pablo laughed and nodded his head.

When they arrived at the apartment, Pablo took Tom to see his room and unpack. In some ways, it wasn't much different from Tom's room back home. There were two beds, a desk, and some toys. He sat down on one of the beds and started bouncing.

"*¿Qué es?*" asked Tom between bounces.

"*Es una cama*," answered Pablo with great amusement.

"S **oo**-nah **kah**-mah," repeated Tom.

Tom kept pointing to things around the room and asking Pablo what they were called in Spanish.

Pablo eagerly answered his questions.

Do you understand what he is saying in Spanish? Help Tom find the object Pablo is talking about.

Tom started to unpack his suitcase. He took out his baseball and bat, then handed them to Pablo.

"*¿Qué es esto, Tom?*"

"*Es un baseball*," answered Tom proudly. "You mean to tell me you've never played baseball? Why, baseball is the greatest game in the whole wide world! See my cap, the Chicago Cubs, that's my team!"

Pablo looked a little confused. Although he knew about baseball, he preferred other sports.

Pablo reached under his bed and pulled out a soccer ball.

Showing it to Tom, he said, "*Es una pelota de fútbol.*"

"No! That's not a football, Es un soccer ball!" Tom groaned. He was really mixed up. His cousin didn't even know the difference between a soccer ball and a football.

"In Mexico, *fútbol* is a very popular sport. I think you say 'soccer' in America," said a man leaning against the bedroom door.

"*Papá*," cried Pablo. "*¡Este es Tom!*"

"You must be my uncle Juan," said Tom excitedly. "*Buenos días, Tío Juan. ¿Qué tal?*"

"*Buenos días, Tom.* I see you two are getting acquainted. Why don't you take your ball and bat and go play in the park before dinner. Pablo will show you around the neighborhood."

Pablo led Tom outside the apartment. Tom was curious to see what a Mexican neighborhood looked like. As they started to walk down the street, he saw a woman pushing a baby carriage.

"*¿Qué es?*" asked Tom.

"*¿Quién es?*" corrected Pablo. "*Es un bebé*," he answered holding up one finger and pointing to the baby.

"Oon beh-**beh**," repeated Tom. "One baby."

Further down the street, Pablo pointed to two policemen dressed in blue uniforms standing on a corner. They looked very important.

"*Son dos policías*."

"Dos po-lee-**C**-ahs," repeated Tom. "Two policemen. Hey Pablo, how do you count to ten in Spanish? You know, one, two, three . . ."

Tom held up ten fingers to help Pablo understand what he wanted.

And he did understand!

Pablo pointed to three cats walking on a fence and said "*tres gatos*."

"Trehs **gah**-tos," repeated Tom. "Three cats. *Uno*, *dos*, *tres*."

"*Cuatro árboles*," continued Pablo.

"koo-**ah**-tro **R**-bo-lehs, four trees," sang Tom. He liked this game.

On their way to the park, Pablo taught Tom how to count to ten.

Can you help Tom learn to count?

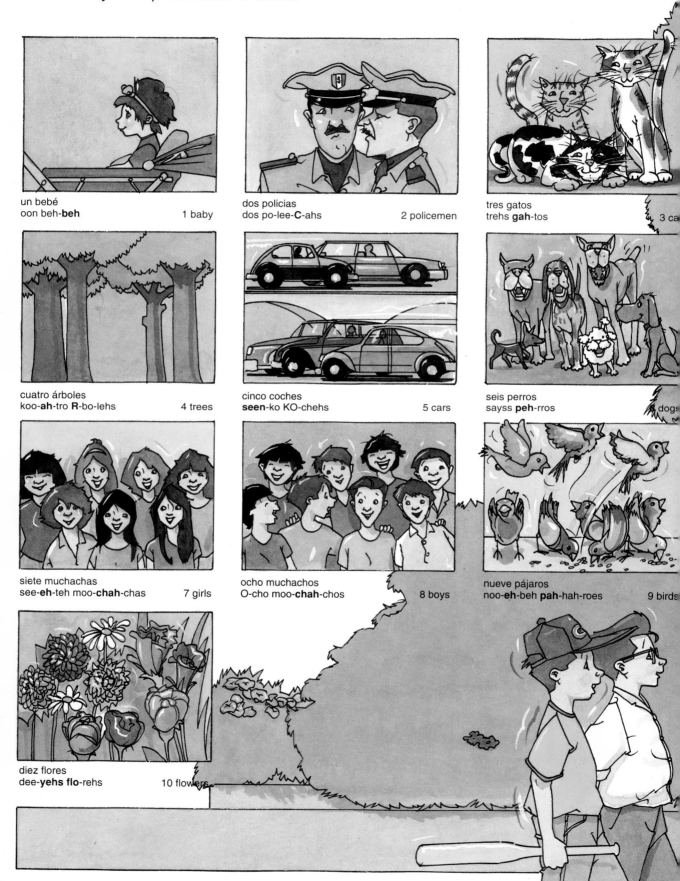

un bebé
oon beh-**beh**
1 baby

dos policias
dos po-lee-**C**-ahs
2 policemen

tres gatos
trehs **gah**-tos
3 cats

cuatro árboles
koo-**ah**-tro **R**-bo-lehs
4 trees

cinco coches
seen-ko KO-chehs
5 cars

seis perros
sayss **peh**-rros
6 dogs

siete muchachas
see-**eh**-teh moo-**chah**-chas
7 girls

ocho muchachos
O-cho moo-**chah**-chos
8 boys

nueve pájaros
noo-**eh**-beh **pah**-hah-roes
9 birds

diez flores
dee-**yehs flo**-rehs
10 flowers

When they arrived at the park, Tom recognized some of the things he had seen with Pablo.

He saw some: *bebés, perros, muchachas, muchachos, gatos, árboles, pájaros, and flores*.

Can you find them too?
How many of each do you see?

Tom and Pablo found an open spot on the grass. Tom took out his baseball bat and gave it to Pablo.

"Now, I'm going to throw the ball. You watch it carefully and try to hit it," explained Tom.

Pablo didn't look too sure of himself, but nodded just the same.
He bravely lifted the bat.

Tom threw the ball and . . .

. . . Pablo missed.

"*Lo siento, Tom*," said Pablo turning red. He was really discouraged.

"Don't be sorry, we'll try again. You can do it! You're my cousin, aren't you!" said Tom.

Tom threw another ball, and another, and another.

Finally, Pablo hit one . . .

. . . smack into a flower bed!

"Good hit!" yelled Tom jumping up and down. "Your aim is a little off, but it was a great first try."

"¡*Gracias, Tom!*" replied Pablo.

Both boys walked to the flower bed.

"I see it! It's over here, next to the red flowers," indicated Tom.

"*No Tom, las flores amarillas,*" insisted Pablo standing near some yellow flowers.

"¿Qué es lahs **flo**-rehs ah-mah-**ree**-yahs?" asked Tom.

Pablo picked some yellow flowers and handed them to Tom.

"Ah, I get it, *flores* means flowers and *amarillas* means yellow," said Tom excitedly.

And these?" asked Tom, bending down to pick some red flowers.

"*Las flores rojas*," answered Pablo.

"ro-has, red, *rojas*," repeated Tom. "And these other colors—white, green, orange, blue, and violet? How do you say them in Spanish?" Tom's bunch of flowers was growing bigger and bigger.

"*Blancas, verdes, anaranjadas, azules, y violetas*," explained Pablo.

"**Blan**-cas, **vehr**-des, ah-nah-rahn-**hah**-das, ah-**sool**-ehs, V-O-**leh**-tahs—why violetas is almost the same as violet in English!"

"I found it!" cried Tom holding up the lost baseball.

But Pablo wasn't listening. He was looking over Tom's shoulder at something and seemed pretty worried about what he saw.

"*¿Qué pasa?*" a voice boomed out.

Tom turned around and found himself standing face to face with *un policia*.

"*Lo siento, señor policía,*" said Pablo nervously.

"*Lo siento*, seh-**nyor** *policía,*" repeated Tom, trying to hide the flowers behind his back. "But you see we were playing baseball, and my cousin hit the ball too hard, and . . ."

El señor policía did not seem impressed.

Suddenly, Tom had an idea.

"*Es un regalo*," he said holding out the bunch of flowers to the policeman. Then Tom put on his best smile, the one that always worked when he got in trouble at home.

El señor policía took the flowers and scratched his head. Just as he opened his mouth to speak, Tom grabbed Pablo by the sleeve and started to back away.

"*Adiós, señor*," yelled Tom.

And with that, the two boys ran out of the park.

Outside the apartment, they stopped to catch their breath. Luckily, the policeman wasn't following them.

"Did you see the look on his face when I gave him the flowers?" Tom imitated *el señor policía* for Pablo.

Pablo took one look at Tom and burst out laughing. Soon both boys were in hysterics.

Inside the apartment, *Tía Margarita* sent Tom and Pablo to their room to get ready for dinner.

Tom felt happy. He was having a great time in Mexico City and Pablo really wasn't that different from his friends back home after all. It didn't matter that Tom couldn't speak Spanish very well, and that Pablo couldn't speak English. They were still friends.

Tom took off his baseball cap and handed it to Pablo.

"*Es un regalo.*"

"*¿Para mí? ¡Ay Tom, gracias!*" exclaimed Pablo.

The two boys stood side by side in front of a mirror while Pablo took off his glasses and tried on his new cap.

But wait a minute! Who is who? That's not Pablo anymore. The baseball cap had transformed Pablo into Tom!

Tom had another great idea. "Pablo, let's play a joke on your mom and dad!"

He took off his shirt and handed it to Pablo. "Now give me your shirt."

Pablo slowly began to smile. He understood what Tom wanted him to do.

"¡A la mesa! Dinner's ready!" called *Tía Margarita* from the dining room.

Five minutes later both boys walked into the dining room.

"Tom, you sit here next to me," said *Tia Margarita*.

She turned to Pablo and explained something to him quickly in Spanish.

Pablo didn't move. He just stood there smiling.

"Pablo, please do what your mother asked," said *Tío Juan*. He was getting rather annoyed.

Both boys suddenly started to laugh.

"*Mamá, Papá, es Tom*," explained the fake Tom pointing to the real Tom.

"I'm not Pablo, *Tía Margarita y Tío Juan*, I'm Tom! That's Pablo, he's just wearing my clothes!" shouted the fake Pablo pointing to the real Pablo. "We really fooled you, didn't we?"

Tía Margarita and Tío Juan started to laugh too. "Well, Tom, it looks like you're practically Mexican now."

"No, I'm not. I'm American!" said Tom, "but I'm learning Spanish fast!"

After dinner, Tom phoned his mom,

"Mexico City is great, Mom. I saw
Paseo de la Reforma today. And I learned how to
count to ten, and the names of colors.
And we played baseball in the
park. And Mom, you were right about
Pablo. He's not so different from me.
I understand him, even if I don't know
how to say lots of things in Spanish .
But he's teaching me. I gotta go now . . .
I love you too, Mom.

Adiós! "

Guide to Spanish Pronunciation

Pronouncing Spanish isn't always easy! That's why Tom must repeat every Spanish word he hears. Whenever possible, he uses English words that sound the same as the Spanish word to help him speak Spanish like Pablo. Here is the "secret code" that Tom uses for representing the correct sound in Spanish.

• For any letter or group of letters that you see printed in boldface—that is, darker than the others—use a louder voice.
> Example: *gatos* **gah**—tos

• When you see a capital letter, pronounce it as if you were reciting the English alphabet.
> Example: *árboles* **R**-bo-lehs

• In Spanish, the combinations **ch** and **ll** make up two additional alphabet letters. The **ñ** is also another letter. You can pronounce them by using similar English sounds:

> **ch** Pronounce it as the English "ch" in "chocolate."
> > Example: *muchacha* moo-**cha**-cha

> **ll** Pronounce it like the English "y" in "year."
> > Example: *silla* **C**-yah

> **ñ** Pronounce it by joining the sounds of two English letters, "ny."
> > Example: *señor* seh-**nyor**

• Keep in mind that in Spanish the j sounds like the English "h" in "hat."
> Example: *anaranjadas* ah-nah-rahn-**hah**-das

• Pronounce the **r** at the beginning of a Spanish word and the double **rr** in the middle of some Spanish words with a stronger sound than you use for the English "r." This Spanish sound is almost like the purring of a cat.
> Examples: *regalo* reh-**gah**-lo
> *perros* **peh**-rros

Glossary (Spanish-English)

Spanish	Pronunciation	English
A		
Aeropuerto	air-O-**poo-ehr**-toe	Airport
¡A la mesa!	ah lah **meh**-sah	Dinner is ready!
Adiós	ah-D-**os**	Good bye
Amarillas	ah-mah-**ree**-yahs	Yellow (plural)
Anaranjadas	ah-nah-rahn-**hah**-das	Orange (plural)
Apellido	ah-peh-**yee**-doe	Surname
Apellido de soltera	ah-peh-**yee**-doe deh sol-**teh**-rah	Maiden Name
Árboles	**R**-bo-lehs	Trees
Avión	ah-V-**on**	Plane
Ay	**I**	Oh
Azules	ah-**sool**-ehs	Blue (plural)

B

Bandera	bahn-**deh**-rah	Flag
Bebé	beh-**beh**	Baby
Bebés	beh-**behs**	Babies
Bien	B-N	Fine
Bienvenido	B-N-veh-**nee**-doe	Welcome
Blancas	**blan**-cas	White (plural)
Buenos días	boo-**eh**-nos D-ahs	Good day

C

Cama	**kah**-mah	Bed
Cinco	**seen**-ko	Five
Cuatro	koo-**ah**-tro	Four

D

De	deh	Of
Diez	D-**S**	Ten
Dirección	D-rehk-C-**on**	Direction
Domicilio	doe-me-**C**-lee-oh	Address
Dos	dos	Two

E

El	L	The (masculine)
Embarque	M-**bar**-K	Embarkation
Es	S	Is
Escritorio	S-cree-**toe**-ree-o	Desk
Esto	**S**-toe	This (masculine)

F

Fecha	**feh**-chah	Date
Flores	**flo**-rehs	Flowers
Fútbol	foot-ball	Soccer

G

Gatos	**gah**-tos	Cats
Gracias	**grah**-C-ahs	Thank you

H

Hola	**O**-lah	Hi

J

Juguete	hoo-**geh**-teh	Toy

L

La	lah	The (feminine)
Las	lahs	The (plural)
Libro	**lee**-bro	Book
Lo siento	lo **C-N**-toe	I am sorry

M

Mamá	mah-**mah**	Momma
Mesa	**meh**-sah	Table
Muchachas	moo-**chah**-chas	Girls
Muchachos	moo-**chah**-chos	Boys

N

Nacimiento	nah-C-**me**-**N**-toe	Birth
Nacionalidad	nah-C-O-nah-lee-**dad**	Nationality
No	no	No
Nombres	**nom**-brehs	Names
Nueve	noo-**eh**-veh	Nine

O

Ocupación	o-coop-ah-**C-on**	Occupation
Ocho	**o**-cho	Eight

P

Pájaros	**pah**-ha-roes	Birds
Papá	pah-**pah**	Poppa
¿Para mí?	pah-rah **me**	For me?
Paseo de la Reforma	pah-**seh**-O deh lah reh-**for**-mah	Reforma Drive
Pelota de fútbol	peh-**lo**-tah deh foot-ball	Soccer ball
Perros	**peh**-rros	Dogs
Policía	po-lee-**C-ah**	Policeman
Policías	po-lee-**C-ahs**	Policemen
Por favor	**pore**-fah-vore	Please
Primo	**pree**-mo	Cousin

Q

¿Qué es?	K S	What is it?
¿Qué es esto?	K S **S**-toe	What is this?
¿Qué pasa?	K **pah**-sah	What is going on?
¿Qué tal?	**K** tahl	How is it going?
¿Quién es?	key-**N** S	Who is it?

R

Regalo	reh-**gah**-lo	Present
Rojas	**ro**-has	Red (plural)

S

Seis	sayss	Six
Señor	seh-**nyor**	Mister, sir
Sí	see	Yes
Silla	**C**-yah	Chair
Son	son	They are

T

Tarjeta de desembarque	tar-**heh**-tah deh des-M-**bar**-K	Disembarkation card
Tía	**T**-ah	Aunt
Tío	**T**-O	Uncle
Tres	trehs	Three

U

Un	oon	A (masculine)
Una	**oo**-nah	A (feminine)
Uno	**oo**-no	One

V

Ventana	vehn-**tah**-nah	window
Verdes	**vehr**-des	Green (plural)
Violetas	V-O-**Leh**-tahs	Violet (plural)

Y

Y	E	And

© Copyright 1994 by Barron's Educational Series, Inc.

All rights reserved.
No part of this book may be reproduced in any form by photostat, microfilm, xerography, or any other means, or incorporated into any information retrieval system, electronic or mechanical, without the written permission of the copyright owner.

All inquiries should be addressed to:
Barron's Educational Series, Inc.
250 Wireless Boulevard
Hauppauge, NY 11788

International Standard Book No.   0-8120-6374-0 (hardcover)
                                   0-8120-1388-3 (paperback)

Library of Congress Catalog Card No. 93-49851

Library of Congress Cataloging-in-Publication Data

Bovaird, Anne Elizabeth.
    Goodbye USA—hola México! / Anne Elizabeth Bovaird :
Spanish version by Harriet Barnett ; illustrated
by Pierre Ballouhey.
        p.   cm.—(A Language learning adventure)
    Summary: Tom's mother teaches him a few essential words in Spanish
before he visits relatives in Mexico and he learns even more words
during his stay. Pronunciation information is included in the text.
    ISBN 0-8120-6374-0.—ISBN 0-8120-1388-3 (pbk.)
    [1. Spanish language—Fiction. 2. Mexico—Fiction. 3. Cousins—
Fiction.] I. Ballouhey, Pierre, ill. II. Title. III. Series.
PZ7.B6716Go   1994
[Fic]—dc20   93-49851
                                                  CIP
                                                  AC

PRINTED IN HONG KONG
4567   9955   987654321

HP BR
J
BOVAIRD
A

BOSTON PUBLIC LIBRARY

3 9999 03621 597 6

3/2000

Hyde Park Branch Library
35 Harvard Avenue
Hyde Park, MA 02136

GAYLORD F